A Beginning-to-Read Book

Merry Christmas, Dear Dragon

by Margaret Hillert
Illustrated by Jack Pullan

NORWOOD HOUSE PRESS

DEAR CAREGIVER,

The books in this Beginning-to-Read collection may look somewhat familiar in that the original versions could have been a part of your own early reading experiences. These carefully written texts feature common sight words to provide your child multiple exposures to the words appearing most frequently in written text. These new versions have been updated and the engaging illustrations are highly appealing to a contemporary audience of young readers.

Begin by reading the story to your child, followed by letting him or her read familiar words and soon your child will be able to read the story independently. At each step of the way, be sure to praise your reader's efforts to build his or her confidence as an independent reader. Discuss the pictures and encourage your child to make connections between the story and his or her own life. At the end of the story, you will find reading activities and a word list that will help your child practice and strengthen beginning reading skills. These activities, along with the comprehension questions are aligned to current standards, so reading efforts at home will directly support the instructional goals in the classroom.

Above all, the most important part of the reading experience is to have fun and enjoy it!

Shannon Cannon

Shannon Cannon,
Literacy Consultant

Norwood House Press • www.norwoodhousepress.com
Beginning-to-Read™ is a registered trademark of Norwood House Press.
Illustration and cover design copyright ©2017 by Norwood House Press. All Rights Reserved.

Authorized adapted reprint from the U.S. English language edition, entitled Merry Christmas, Dear Dragon by Margaret Hillert. Copyright © 2017 Margaret Hillert. Reprinted with permission. All rights reserved. Pearson and Merry Christmas, Dear Dragon are trademarks, in the US and/or other countries, of Pearson Education, Inc. or its affiliates. This publication is protected by copyright, and prior permission to re-use in any way in any format is required by both Norwood House Press and Pearson Education. This book is authorized in the United States for use in schools and public libraries.

LIBRARY OF CONGRESS CATALOGING-IN-PUBLICATION DATA

Names: Hillert, Margaret, author. I Pullan, Jack, illustrator.
Title: Merry Christmas, Dear Dragon / by Margaret Hillert ; illustrated by Jack Pullan.
Description: Chicago, IL : Norwood House Press, [2016] I Series: A
   beginning-to-read book I Summary: "A boy and his pet dragon enjoy winter
   activities and prepare for a merry Christmas. Completely re-illustrated
   from original edition. Includes reading activities and a word list"–
   Provided by publisher.
Identifiers: LCCN 2015046744 (print) I LCCN 2016014728 (ebook) I ISBN
   9781599537757 (library edition : alk. paper) I ISBN 9781603579018 (eBook)
Subjects: I CYAC: Winter--Fiction. I Christmas--Fiction. I Dragons--Fiction.
Classification: LCC PZ7.H558 Me 2016 (print) I LCC PZ7.H558 (ebook) I DDC
   [E]--dc23
LC record available at http://lccn.loc.gov/2015046744

288N—072016
Manufactured in the United States of America in North Mankato, Minnesota.

Look at this.
Down, down it comes.
What fun.
What fun.

But it is work, too.
I will have to work.
I can make it go away.

Oh, my.
Look at you.
You can help me.
What a big help you are.

We can play, too.
It is fun to play in this.
Run, run, run.
And jump, jump, jump.

We can make something big.
Big, big, big.
See, see.
It looks like you!

Oh, oh.
Look at that car.
It can not go.

You can help.
Work, work, work.
Now it can go away.
That is good.

Now come with me.
We have to get something.
Something for the house.

Look here. Look here.
Here is the one we want.
Not too little.
Not too big.

Mother, Mother.
See me ride.
Look what we have.
It is for the house.

I see it.
I like it.
It is a good one.
Come in.
Come in.

See what we can make.
Cookies. Cookies.
Look at this!

One for me.
And one for you.
A big, big one for you!

Now we will do this.
Here are some balls.
This is fun.
I like to do this.

You can help with this one.
Make it go up.
Up, up, up.

Where are you now?
Where did you go?
I can not guess.
I can not find you.

Come here. Come here.
I want you.
I like you here with me.

Oh, here you are!
I see you now.
Look at you.
You are funny.

You can help with this, too.
I can not make it work.
You will have to do it for me.

Oh, my.
Oh, my.
Look at it now.
Red and yellow.
I like this.

Here you are with me.
And here I am with you.
Oh, what a merry Christmas,
Dear Dragon.

The following activities support the findings of the National Reading Panel that determined the most effective components for reading instruction are: Phonemic Awareness, Phonics, Vocabulary, Fluency, and Text Comprehension.

Phonemic Awareness: The /m/ sound

Oddity Task: Say the /m/ sound for your child. Read each word below to your child and ask your child to say the word without the /**m**/ sound:

mad - /m/ = ad	moat - /m/ = oat	mice - /m/ = ice
man - /m/ = an	mend - /m/ = end	mill - /m/ = ill
meat - /m/ = eat	mat - /m/ = at	

Phonics: The letter Mm

1. Demonstrate how to form the letters **M** and **m** for your child.

2. Have your child practice writing **M** and **m** at least three times each.

3. Ask your child to point to the words in the book that begin with the letter **m**.

4. Write down the following words and ask your child to circle the letter **m** in each word:

merry	make	yam	comb	my	jam
mother	moon	farm	me	tummy	from
tumble	room	make	map	camp	mom

Vocabulary: Concept Words

1. Fold a piece of paper vertically in half.

2. Draw a line down the fold to divide the paper in two parts.

3. Write the words work and play in separate columns at the top of the page.

4. Write the following statements on separate pieces of paper:

shoveling snow	riding a sled	building a snowman
baking cookies	cleaning house	emptying the garbage
watching movies	using the computer	picking up toys

5. Read each statement aloud and ask your child whether the action belongs in the work or play column. (Note: some may be considered work and play, depending on the situation.)

6. Invite your child to tell you why he or she has chosen the column.

Fluency: Choral Reading

1. Reread the story with your child at least two more times while your child tracks the print by running a finger under the words as they are read. Ask your child to read the words he or she knows with you.

2. Reread the story aloud together. Be careful to read at a rate that your child can keep up with.

3. Repeat choral reading and allow your child to be the lead reader and ask him or her to change from a whisper to a loud voice while you follow along and change your voice.

Text Comprehension: Discussion Time

1. Ask your child to retell the sequence of events in the story.

2. To check comprehension, ask your child the following questions:
   - Why couldn't the car go on page 9?
   - What is your favorite part of the story? Why?
   - What are some of the things your family does to celebrate Christmas?
   - If your family celebrates another winter holiday, how do you celebrate?

WORD LIST

Merry Christmas, Dear Dragon uses the 70 words listed below.

This list can be used to practice reading the words that appear in the text. You may wish to write the words on index cards and use them to help your child build automatic word recognition. Regular practice with these words will enhance your child's fluency in reading connected text.

a	dear	I	oh	up
am	did	in	one	
and	do	is		want
are	down	it	play	we
at	dragon			what
away		jump	red	where
	find		ride	will
balls	for	like	run	with
big	fun	little		work
but	funny	look(s)	see	
			some	yellow
can	get	make	something	you
car	go	me		
Christmas	good	merry	that	
come(s)	guess	Mother	the	
cookies		my	this	
	have		to	
	help	not	too	
	here	now		
	house			

ABOUT THE AUTHOR Margaret Hillert has helped millions of children all over the world learn to read independently. She was a first grade teacher for 34 years and during that time started writing books that her students could both gain confidence in reading and enjoy. She wrote well over 100 books for children just learning to read. As a child, she enjoyed writing poetry and continued her poetic writings as an adult for both children and adults.

Photograph by Glenna Washburn

ABOUT THE ILLUSTRATOR A talented and creative illustrator, Jack Pullan, is a graduate of William Jewell College. He has also studied informally at Oxford University and the Kansas City Art Institute. He was mentored by the renowned watercolor artists, Jim Hamil and Bill Amend. Jack's work has graced the pages of many enjoyable children's books, various educational materials, cartoon strips, as well as many greeting cards. Jack currently resides in Kansas.